The Bedford-Row Conspiracy by William Makepeace Thackeray

The great author of Vanity Fair and The Luck Of Barry Lyndon was born in India in 1811.

At age 5 his father died and his mother sent him back to England. His education was of the best but he himself seemed unable to apply his talents to a rigorous work ethic.

However, once he harnessed his talents the works flowed in novels, articles, short stories, sketches and lectures.

Sadly, his personal life was rather more difficult. After a few years of marriage his wife began to suffer from depression and over the years became detached from reality. Thackeray himself suffered from ill health later in his life and the one pursuit that kept him moving forward was that of writing. In his life time, he was placed second only to Dickens. High praise indeed.

Index of Contents

CHAPTER I

OF THE LOVES OF MR. PERKINS AND MISS GORGON, AND OF THE TWO GREAT FACTIONS IN THE TOWN OF OLDBOROUGH

"My dear John," cried Lucy, with a very wise look indeed, "it must and shall be so. As for Doughty Street, with our means, a house is out of the question. We must keep three servants, and Aunt Biggs says the taxes are one-and-twenty pounds a year."

"I have seen a sweet place at Chelsea," remarked John: "Paradise Row, No. 17,—garden—greenhouse— fifty pounds a year—omnibus to town within a mile."

"What! that I may be left alone all day, and you spend a fortune in driving backward and forward in those horrid breakneck cabs? My darling, I should die there—die of fright, I know I should. Did you not say yourself that the road was not as yet lighted, and that the place swarmed with public-houses and dreadful tipsy Irish bricklayers? Would you kill me, John?"

"My da-arling," said John, with tremendous fondness, clutching Miss Lucy suddenly round the waist, and rapping the hand of that young person violently against his waistcoat,—"My da-arling, don't say such things, even in a joke. If I objected to the chambers, it is only because you, my love, with your birth and connections, ought to have a house of your own. The chambers are quite large enough and certainly quite good enough for me." And so, after some more sweet parley on the part of these young people, it was agreed that they should take up their abode, when married, in a part of the House number One hundred and something, Bedford Row.

It will be necessary to explain to the reader that John was no other than John Perkins, Esquire, of the Middle Temple, barrister-at-law, and that Miss Lucy was the daughter of the late Captain Gorgon, and Marianne Biggs, his wife. The Captain being of noble connections, younger son of a baronet, cousin to Lord X—, and related to the Y— family, had angered all his relatives by marrying a very silly pretty young woman, who kept a ladies'-school at Canterbury. She had six hundred pounds to her fortune, which the Captain laid out in the purchase of a sweet travelling-carriage and dressing-case for himself; and going abroad with his lady, spent several years in the principal prisons of Europe, in one of which he died. His wife and daughter were meantime supported by the contributions of Mrs. Jemima Biggs, who still kept the ladies'-school.

At last a dear old relative—such a one as one reads of in romances—died and left seven thousand pounds apiece to the two sisters, whereupon the elder gave up schooling and retired to London; and the younger managed to live with some comfort and decency at Brussels, upon two hundred and ten pounds per annum. Mrs. Gorgon never touched a shilling of her capital, for the very good reason that it was placed entirely out of her reach; so that when she died, her daughter found herself in possession of a sum of money that is not always to be met with in this world.

Her aunt the baronet's lady, and her aunt the ex-schoolmistress, both wrote very pressing invitations to her, and she resided with each for six months after her arrival in England. Now, for a second time, she had come to Mrs. Biggs, Caroline Place, Mecklenburgh Square. It was under the roof of that respectable old lady that John Perkins, Esquire, being invited to take tea, wooed and won Miss Gorgon.

Having thus described the circumstances of Miss Gorgon's life, let us pass for a moment from that young lady, and lift up the veil of mystery which envelopes the deeds and character of Perkins.

Perkins, too, was an orphan; and he and his Lucy, of summer evenings, when Sol descending lingered fondly yet about the minarets of the Foundling, and gilded the grassplots of Mecklenburgh Square— Perkins, I say, and Lucy would often sit together in the summer-house of that pleasure-ground, and muse upon the strange coincidences of their life. Lucy was motherless and fatherless; so too was Perkins. If Perkins was brotherless and sisterless, was not Lucy likewise an only child? Perkins was twenty-three: his age and Lucy's united, amounted to forty-six; and it was to be remarked, as a fact still more extraordinary, that while Lucy's relatives were AUNTS, John's were UNCLES. Mysterious spirit of love! let us treat thee with respect and whisper not too many of thy secrets. The fact is, John and Lucy were a pair of fools (as every young couple OUGHT to be who have hearts that are worth a farthing), and were ready to find coincidences, sympathies, hidden gushes of feeling, mystic unions of the soul, and what not, in every single circumstance that occurred from the rising of the sun to the going down thereof, and in the intervals. Bedford Row, where Perkins lived, is not very far from Mecklenburgh Square; and John used to say that he felt a comfort that his house and Lucy's were served by the same muffin-man.

Further comment is needless. A more honest, simple, clever, warm-hearted, soft, whimsical, romantical, high-spirited young fellow than John Perkins did not exist. When his father, Doctor Perkins, died, this, his only son, was placed under the care of John Perkins, Esquire, of the house of Perkins, Scully, and Perkins, those celebrated attorneys in the trading town of Oldborough, which the second partner, William Pitt Scully, Esquire, represented in Parliament and in London.

All John's fortune was the house in Bedford Row, which, at his father's death, was let out into chambers, and brought in a clear hundred a year. Under his uncle's roof at Oldborough, where he lived with thirteen red-haired male and female cousins, he was only charged fifty pounds for board, clothes, and pocket-money, and the remainder of his rents was carefully put by for him until his majority. When he approached that period—when he came to belong to two spouting-clubs at Oldborough, among the young merchants and lawyers'-clerks—to blow the flute nicely, and play a good game at billiards—to have written one or two smart things in the Oldborough Sentinel—to be fond of smoking (in which act he was discovered by his fainting aunt at three o'clock one morning)—in one word, when John Perkins arrived at manhood, he discovered that he was quite unfit to be an attorney, that he detested all the ways of his uncle's stern, dull, vulgar, regular, red-headed family, and he vowed that he would go to London and make his fortune. Thither he went, his aunt and cousins, who were all "serious," vowing that he was a lost boy; and when his history opens, John had been two years in the metropolis, inhabiting his own garrets; and a very nice compact set of apartments, looking into the back-garden, at this moment falling vacant, the prudent Lucy Gorgon had visited them, and vowed that she and her John should there commence housekeeping.

All these explanations are tedious, but necessary; and furthermore, it must be said, that as John's uncle's partner was the Liberal member for Oldborough, so Lucy's uncle was its Ministerial representative.

This gentleman, the brother of the deceased Captain Gorgon, lived at the paternal mansion of Gorgon Castle, and rejoiced in the name and title of Sir George Grimsby Gorgon.

He, too, like his younger brother, had married a lady beneath his own rank in life; having espoused the daughter and heiress of Mr. Hicks, the great brewer at Oldborough, who held numerous mortgages on the Gorgon property, all of which he yielded up, together with his daughter Juliana, to the care of the baronet.

What Lady Gorgon was in character, this history will show. In person, if she may be compared to any vulgar animal, one of her father's heavy, healthy, broad-flanked, Roman-nosed white dray-horses might, to the poetic mind, appear to resemble her. At twenty she was a splendid creature, and though not at her full growth, yet remarkable for strength and sinew; at forty-five she was as fine a woman as any in His Majesty's dominions. Five feet seven in height, thirteen stone, her own teeth and hair, she looked as if she were the mother of a regiment of Grenadier Guards. She had three daughters of her own size, and at length, ten years after the birth of the last of the young ladies, a son—one son—George Augustus Frederick Grimsby Gorgon, the godson of a royal duke, whose steady officer in waiting Sir George had been for many years.

It is needless to say, after entering so largely into a description of Lady Gorgon, that her husband was a little shrivelled wizen-faced creature, eight inches shorter than her Ladyship. This is the way of the world, as every single reader of this book must have remarked; for frolic love delights to join giants and pigmies of different sexes in the bonds of matrimony. When you saw her Ladyship in flame-coloured satin and gorgeous toque and feathers, entering the drawing-room, as footmen along the stairs shouted melodiously, "Sir George and Lady Gorgon," you beheld in her company a small withered old gentleman, with powder and large royal household buttons, who tripped at her elbow as a little weak-legged colt does at the side of a stout mare.

The little General had been present at about a hundred and twenty pitched battles on Hounslow Heath and Wormwood Scrubs, but had never drawn his sword against an enemy. As might be expected, therefore, his talk and tenue were outrageously military. He had the whole Army List by heart—that is, as far as the field-officers: all below them he scorned. A bugle at Gorgon Castle always sounded at breakfast, and dinner: a gun announced sunset. He clung to his pigtail for many years after the army had forsaken that ornament, and could never be brought to think much of the Peninsular men for giving it up. When he spoke of the Duke, he used to call him "MY LORD WELLINGTON—I RECOLLECT HIM AS CAPTAIN WELLESLEY." He swore fearfully in conversation, was most regular at church, and regularly read to his family and domestics the morning and evening prayer; he bullied his daughters, seemed to bully his wife, who led him whither she chose; gave grand entertainments, and never asked a friend by chance; had splendid liveries, and starved his people; and was as dull, stingy, pompous, insolent, cringing, ill-tempered a little creature as ever was known.

With such qualities you may fancy that he was generally admired in society and by his country. So he was: and I never knew a man so endowed whose way through life was not safe—who had fewer pangs of conscience—more positive enjoyments—more respect shown to him—more favours granted to him, than such a one as my friend the General.

Her Ladyship was just suited to him, and they did in reality admire each other hugely. Previously to her marriage with the baronet, many love-passages had passed between her and William Pitt Scully, Esquire, the attorney; and there was especially one story, a propos of certain syllabubs and Sally-Lunn cakes, which seemed to show that matters had gone very far. Be this as it may, no sooner did the General (Major Gorgon he was then) cast an eye on her, than Scully's five years' fabric of love was instantly dashed to the ground. She cut him pitilessly, cut Sally Scully, his sister, her dearest friend and confidante, and bestowed her big person upon the little aide-de-camp at the end of a fortnight's wooing. In the course of time their mutual fathers died; the Gorgon estates were unencumbered: patron of both the seats in the borough of Oldborough, and occupant of one, Sir George Grimsby Gorgon, Baronet, was a personage of no small importance.

He was, it scarcely need to be said, a Tory; and this was the reason why William Pitt Scully, Esquire, of the firm of Perkins and Scully, deserted those principles in which he had been bred and christened; deserted that church which he had frequented, for he could not bear to see Sir George and my Lady flaunting in their grand pew;—deserted, I say, the church, adopted the conventicle, and became one of the most zealous and eloquent supporters that Freedom has known in our time. Scully, of the house of Scully and Perkins, was a dangerous enemy. In five years from that marriage, which snatched from the jilted solicitor his heart's young affections, Sir George Gorgon found that he must actually spend seven hundred pounds to keep his two seats. At the next election, a Liberal was set up against his man, and actually ran him hard; and finally, at the end of eighteen years, the rejected Scully—the mean attorney—was actually the FIRST Member for Oldborough, Sir George Grimsby Gorgon, Baronet, being only the second!

The agony of that day cannot be imagined—the dreadful curses of Sir George, who saw fifteen hundred a year robbed from under his very nose—the religious resignation of my Lady—the hideous window-smashing that took place at the "Gorgon Arms," and the discomfiture of the pelted Mayor and Corporation. The very next Sunday, Scully was reconciled to the church (or attended it in the morning, and the meeting twice in the afternoon), and as Doctor Snorter uttered the prayer for the High Court of Parliament, his eye, the eye of his whole party—turned towards Lady Gorgon and Sir George in a most unholy triumph. Sir George (who always stood during prayers, like a military man) fairly sank down among the hassocks, and Lady Gorgon was heard to sob as audibly as ever did little beadle-belaboured urchin.

Scully, when at Oldborough, came from that day forth to church. "What," said he, "was it to him? were we not all brethren?" Old Perkins, however, kept religiously to the Squaretoes congregation. In fact, to tell the truth, this subject had been debated between the partners, who saw the advantage of courting both the Establishment and the Dissenters—a manoeuvre which, I need not say, is repeated in almost every country town in England, where a solicitor's house has this kind of power and connection.

Three months after this election came the races at Oldborough, and the race-ball. Gorgon was so infuriated by his defeat, that he gave "the Gorgon cup and cover," a matter of fifteen pounds. Scully, "although anxious," as he wrote from town, "anxious beyond measure to preserve the breed of horses for which our beloved country has ever been famous, could attend no such sports as these, which but too often degenerated into vice." It was voted a shabby excuse. Lady Gorgon was radiant in her barouche and four, and gladly became the patroness of the ball that was to ensue; and which all the gentry and townspeople, Tory and Whig, were in the custom of attending. The ball took place on the last day of the races. On that day, the walls of the market-house, the principal public buildings, and the "Gorgon Arms Hotel" itself, were plastered with the following:—

"Letter from our distinguished representative, William P. Scully, Esquire, etc., etc.

"HOUSE OF COMMONS: June 1, 18—.

"MY DEAR HEELTAP,—You know my opinion about horseracing, and though I blame neither you nor any brother Englishman who enjoys that manly sport, you will, I am sure, appreciate the conscientious motives which induce me not to appear among my friends and constituents on the festival of the 3rd, 4th, and 5th instant. If I, however, cannot allow my name to appear among your list of stewards, ONE at least of the representatives of Oldborough has no such scruples. Sir George Gorgon is among you: and though I differ from that honourable Baronet on more than ONE VITAL POINT, I am glad to think that he is with you. A gentleman, a soldier, a man of property in the county, how can he be better employed than in forwarding the county's amusements, and in forwarding the happiness of all?

"Had I no such scruples as those to which I have just alluded, I must still have refrained from coming among you. Your great Oldborough common-drainage and inclosure bill comes on to-morrow, and I shall be AT MY POST. I am sure, if Sir George Gorgon were here, he and I should on this occasion vote side by side, and that party strife would be forgotten in the object of our common interest—OUR DEAR NATIVE TOWN.

"There is, however, another occasion at hand, in which I shall be proud to meet him. Your ball is on the night of the 6th. Party forgotten—brotherly union—innocent mirth—beauty, OUR DEAR TOWN'S BEAUTY, our daughters in the joy of their expanding loveliness, our matrons in the exquisite contemplation of their children's bliss—can you, can I, can Whig or Tory, can any Briton be indifferent to a scene like this, or refuse to join in this heart-stirring festival? If there BE such let them pardon me—I, for one, my dear Heeltap, will be among you on Friday night—ay, and hereby invite all pretty Tory Misses, who are in want of a partner.

"I am here in the very midst of good things, you know, and we old folks like A SUPPER after a dance. Please to accept a brace of bucks and a turtle, which come herewith. My worthy colleague, who was so liberal last year of his soup to the poor, will not, I trust, refuse to taste a little of Alderman Birch's—'tis offered on my part with hearty goodwill. Hey for the 6th, and vive la joie!

"Ever, my dear Heeltap, your faithful

"W. PITT SCULLY.

"P.S.—Of course this letter is STRICTLY PRIVATE. Say that the venison, etc. came from a WELL-WISHER TO OLDBOROUGH."

This amazing letter was published, in defiance of Mr. Scully's injunctions, by the enthusiastic Heeltap, who said, bluntly, in a preface, "that he saw no reason why Mr. Scully should be ashamed of his action, and he, for his part, was glad to let all friends at Oldborough know of it."

The allusion about the Gorgon soup was killing: thirteen paupers in Oldborough had, it was confidently asserted, died of it. Lady Gorgon, on the reading of this letter, was struck completely dumb; Sir George Gorgon was wild. Ten dozen of champagne was he obliged to send down to the "Gorgon Arms," to be added to the festival. He would have stayed away if he could, but he dared not.

At nine o'clock, he in general's uniform; his wife in blue satin and diamonds; his daughters in blue crape and white roses; his niece, Lucy Gorgon, in white muslin; his son, George Augustus Frederick Grimsby Gorgon, in a blue velvet jacket, sugar-loaf buttons, and nankeens, entered the north door of the ballroom, to much cheering, and the sound of "God save the King!"

At that very same moment, and from the south door, issued William Pitt Scully, Esquire, M.P., and his staff. Mr. Scully had a brand-new blue coat and brass buttons, buff waistcoat, white kerseymere tights, pumps with large rosettes, and pink silk stockings.

"This wool," said he to a friend, "was grown on Oldborough sheep, this cloth was spun in Oldborough looms, these buttons were cast in an Oldborough manufactory, these shoes were made by an Oldborough tradesman, this HEART first beat in Oldborough town, and pray Heaven may be buried there!"

Could anything resist a man like this? John Perkins, who had come down as one of Scully's aides-de-camp, in a fit of generous enthusiasm, leaped on a whist-table, flung up a pocket-handkerchief, and shrieked—"SCULLY FOR EVER!"

Heeltap, who was generally drunk, fairly burst into tears, and the grave tradesmen and Whig gentry, who had dined with the Member at his inn, and accompanied him thence to the "Gorgon Arms," lifted their deep voices and shouted "Hear!" "Good!" "Bravo!" "Noble!" "Scully for ever!" "God bless him!" and "Hurrah!"

The scene was tumultuously affecting; and when young Perkins sprang down from the table and came blushing up to the Member, that gentleman said, "Thank you, Jack! THANK you, my boy! THANK you," in a way which made Perkins think that his supreme cup of bliss was quaffed; that he had but to die: for that life had no other such joy in store for him. Scully was Perkins's Napoleon—he yielded himself up to the attorney, body and soul.

Whilst this scene was going on under one chandelier of the ballroom, beneath the other scarlet little General Gorgon, sumptuous Lady Gorgon, the daughters and niece Gorgons, were standing surrounded by their Tory court, who affected to sneer and titter at the Whig demonstrations which were taking place.

"What a howwid thmell of whithkey!" lisped Cornet Fitch, of the Dragoons, to Miss Lucy, confidentially. "And the—the are what they call Whigth, are they? He! he!"

"They are drunk,—me,—drunk, by—!" said the General to the Mayor.

"Which is Scully?" said Lady Gorgon, lifting her glass gravely (she was at that very moment thinking of the syllabubs). "Is it that tipsy man in the green coat, or that vulgar creature in the blue one?"

"Law, my Lady," said the Mayoress, "have you forgotten him? Why, that's him in blue and buff."

"And a monthous fine man, too," said Cornet Fitch. "I wish we had him in our twoop—he'th thix feet thwee, if he'th an inch; ain't he, Genewal?"

No reply.

"And heavens! Mamma," shrieked the three Gorgons in a breath, "see, one creature is on the whist-table. Oh, the wretch!

"I'm sure he's very good-looking," said Lucy, simply.

Lady Gorgon darted at her an angry look, and was about to say something very contemptuous, when, at that instant, John Perkins's shout taking effect, Master George Augustus Frederick Grimsby Gorgon, not knowing better, incontinently raised a small shout on his side.

"Hear! good! bravo!" exclaimed he; "Scully for ever! Hurra-a-a-ay!" and fell skipping about like the Whigs opposite.

"Silence, you brute you!" groaned Lady Gorgon; and seizing him by the shirt-frill and coat-collar, carried him away to his nurse, who, with many other maids of the Whig and Tory parties, stood giggling and peeping at the landing-place.

Fancy how all these small incidents augmented the heap of Lady Gorgon's anger and injuries! She was a dull phlegmatic woman for the most part, and contented herself generally with merely despising her neighbours; but oh! what a fine active hatred raged in her bosom for victorious Scully! At this moment Mr. Perkins had finished shaking hands with his Napoleon—Napoleon seemed bent upon some tremendous enterprise. He was looking at Lady Gorgon very hard.

"She's a fine woman," said Scully, thoughtfully; he was still holding the hand of Perkins. And then, after a pause, "Gad! I think I'll try."

"Try what, sir?"

"She's a DEUCED fine woman!" burst out again the tender solicitor. "I WILL go. Springer, tell the fiddlers to strike up."

Springer scuttled across the room, and gave the leader of the band a knowing nod. Suddenly, "God save the King" ceased, and "Sir Roger de Coverley" began. The rival forces eyed each other; Mr. Scully, accompanied by his friend, came forward, looking very red, and fumbling two large kid gloves.

"HE'S GOING TO ASK ME TO DANCE," hissed out Lady Gorgon, with a dreadful intuition, and she drew back behind her lord.

"D— it, madam, THEN DANCE with him!" said the General. "Don't you see that the scoundrel is carrying it all his own way! — him! and — him! and — him!" (All of which dashes the reader may fill up with oaths of such strength as may be requisite).

"General!" cried Lady Gorgon, but could say no more. Scully was before her.

"Madam!" exclaimed the Liberal Member for Oldborough, "in a moment like this—I say—that is—that on the present occasion—your Ladyship—unaccustomed as I am—pooh, psha—WILL your Ladyship give me the distinguished honour and pleasure of going down the country-dance with your Ladyship?"

An immense heave of her Ladyship's ample chest was perceptible. Yards of blond lace, which might be compared to a foam of the sea, were agitated at the same moment, and by the same mighty emotion. The river of diamonds which flowed round her Ladyship's neck, seemed to swell and to shine more than ever. The tall plumes on her ambrosial head bowed down beneath the storm. In other words, Lady Gorgon, in a furious rage, which she was compelled to restrain, trembled, drew up, and bowing majestically, said,—

"Sir, I shall have much pleasure." With this, she extended her hand. Scully, trembling, thrust forward one of his huge kid-gloves, and led her to the head of the country-dance. John Perkins—who I presume had been drinking pretty freely, so as to have forgotten his ordinary bashfulness—looked at the three Gorgons in blue, then at the pretty smiling one in white, and stepping up to her, without the smallest hesitation, asked her if she would dance with him.

The young lady smilingly agreed. The great example of Scully and Lady Gorgon was followed by all dancing men and women. Political enmities were forgotten. Whig voters invited Tory voters' wives to the dance. The daughters of Reform accepted the hands of the sons of Conservatism. The reconciliation of the Romans and Sabines was not more touching than this sweet fusion. Whack—whack! Springer clapped his hands; and the fiddlers adroitly obeying the cheerful signal, began playing "Sir Roger de Coverley" louder than ever.

I do not know by what extraordinary charm (nescio qua praeter solitum, etc.), but young Perkins, who all his life had hated country-dances, was delighted with this one, and skipped and laughed, poussetting, crossing, down-the-middling, with his merry little partner, till every one of the bettermost sort of the thirty-nine couples had dropped panting away, and till the youngest Miss Gorgon, coming up to his partner, said in a loud hissing scornful whisper, "Lucy, Mamma thinks you have danced quite enough with this—this person." And Lucy, blushing, starting back, and looking at Perkins in a very melancholy way, made him a little curtsey, and went off to the Gorgonian party with her cousin. Perkins was too frightened to lead her back to her place—too frightened at first, and then too angry. "Person!" said he: his soul swelled with a desperate republicanism: he went back to his patron more of a Radical than ever.

He found that gentleman in the solitary tea-room, pacing up and down before the observant landlady and handmaidens of the "Gorgon Arms," wiping his brows, gnawing his fingers—his ears looming over his stiff white shirt-collar as red as fire. Once more the great man seized John Perkins's hand as the latter came up.

"D— the aristocrats!" roared the ex-follower of Squaretoes.

"And so say I! but what's the matter, sir?"

"What's the matter?—Why, that woman—that infernal, haughty, straitlaced, cold-blooded brewer's daughter! I loved that woman, sir—I KISSED that woman, sir, twenty years ago: we were all but engaged, sir: we've walked for hours and hours, sir—us and the governess—I've got a lock of her hair, sir, among my papers now; and to-night, would you believe it?—as soon as she got to the bottom of the set, away she went—not one word would she speak to me all the way down: and when I wanted to lead her to her place, and asked her if she would have a glass of negus, 'Sir,' says she, 'I have done my duty; I bear no malice: but I consider you a traitor to Sir George Gorgon's family—a traitor and an upstart! I consider your speaking to me as a piece of insolent vulgarity, and beg you will leave me to myself!' There's her speech, sir. Twenty people heard it, and all of her Tory set too. I'll tell you what, Jack: at the next election I'll put YOU up. Oh that woman! that woman!—and to think that I love her still!" Here Mr. Scully paused, and fiercely consoled himself by swallowing three cups of Mrs. Rincer's green tea.

The fact is, that Lady Gorgon's passion had completely got the better of her reason. Her Ladyship was naturally cold, and artificially extremely squeamish; and when this great red-faced enemy of hers looked tenderly at her through his red little eyes, and squeezed her hand and attempted to renew old acquaintance, she felt such an intolerable disgust at his triumph, at his familiarity, and at the remembrance of her own former liking for him, that she gave utterance to the speech above correctly reported. The Tories were delighted with her spirit, and Cornet Fitch, with much glee, told the story to the General; but that officer, who was at whist with some of his friends, flung down his cards, and coming up to his lady, said briefly,—

"Madam, you are a fool!"

"I will NOT stay here to be bearded by that disgusting man!—Mr. Fitch, call my people.—Henrietta, bring Miss Lucy from that linendraper with whom she is dancing. I will not stay, General, once for all."

Henrietta ran—she hated her cousin: Cornet Fitch was departing. "Stop, Fitch," said Sir George, seizing him by the arm. "You are a fool, Lady Gorgon," said he, "and I repeat it—a — fool! This fellow Scully is carrying all before him: he has talked with everybody, laughed with everybody—and you, with your infernal airs—a brewer's daughter, by —, must sit like a queen and not speak to a soul! You've lost me one seat of my borough, with your infernal pride—fifteen hundred a year, by Jove!—and you think you will bully me out of another. No, madam, you SHALL stay, and stay supper too;—and the girls shall dance with every cursed chimney-sweep and butcher in the room: they shall—confound me!"

Her Ladyship saw that it was necessary to submit; and Mr. Springer, the master of the ceremonies, was called, and requested to point out some eligible partners for the young ladies. One went off with a Whig auctioneer; another figured in a quadrille with a very Liberal apothecary; and the third, Miss Henrietta, remained.

"Hallo you, sir!" roared the little General to John Perkins, who was passing by. John turned round and faced him.

"You were dancing with my niece just now—show us your skill now, and dance with one of my daughters. Stand up, Miss Henrietta Gorgon—Mr. What's-your-name?"

"My name," said John, with marked and majestic emphasis, "is PERKINS." And he looked towards Lucy, who dared not look again.

"Miss Gorgon—Mr. Perkins. There, now go and dance."

"Mr. Perkins regrets, madam," said John, making a bow to Miss Henrietta, "that he is not able to dance this evening. I am this moment obliged to look to the supper; but you will find, no doubt, some other PERSON who will have much pleasure."

"Go to —, sir!" screamed the General, starting up, and shaking his cane.

"Calm yourself, dearest George," said Lady Gorgon, clinging fondly to him. Fitch twiddled his moustaches. Miss Henrietta Gorgon stared with open mouth. The silks of the surrounding dowagers rustled—the countenances of all looked grave.

"I will follow you, sir, wherever you please; and you may hear of me whenever you like," said Mr. Perkins, bowing and retiring. He heard little Lucy sobbing in a corner. He was lost at once—lost in love; he felt as if he could combat fifty generals! he never was so happy in his life.

The supper came; but as that meal cost five shillings a head, General Gorgon dismissed the four spinsters of his family homewards in the carriage, and so saved himself a pound. This added to Jack Perkins's wrath; he had hoped to have seen Miss Lucy once more. He was a steward, and, in the General's teeth, would have done his duty. He was thinking how he would have helped her to the most delicate chicken-wings and blancmanges, how he WOULD have made her take champagne. Under the noses of indignant aunt and uncle, what glorious fun it would have been!

Out of place as Mr. Scully's present was, and though Lady Gorgon and her party sneered at the vulgar notion of venison and turtle for supper, all the world at Oldborough ate very greedily of those two substantial dishes; and the Mayor's wife became from that day forth a mortal enemy of the Gorgons: for, sitting near her Ladyship, who refused the proffered soup and meat, the Mayoress thought herself obliged to follow this disagreeable example. She sent away the plate of turtle with a sigh, saying, however, to the baronet's lady, "I thought, mem, that the LORD MAYOR OF LONDON always had turtle to his supper?"

"And what if he didn't, Biddy?" said his Honour the Mayor; "a good thing's a good thing, and here goes!" wherewith he plunged his spoon into the savoury mess. The Mayoress, as we have said, dared not; but she hated Lady Gorgon, and remembered it at the next election.

The pride, in fact, and insolence of the Gorgon party rendered every person in the room hostile to them; so soon as, gorged with meat, they began to find that courage which Britons invariably derive from their victuals. The show of the Gorgon plate seemed to offend the people. The Gorgon champagne was a long time, too, in making its appearance. Arrive, however, it did. The people were waiting for it; the young ladies, not accustomed to that drink, declined pledging their admirers until it was produced; the men, too, despised the bucellas and sherry, and were looking continually towards the door. At last, Mr. Rincer, the landlord, Mr. Hock, Sir George's butler, and sundry others entered the room. Bang! went the corks—fizz the foamy liquor sparkled into all sorts of glasses that were held out for its reception. Mr. Hock helped Sir George and his party, who drank with great gusto; the wine which was administered to the persons immediately around Mr. Scully was likewise pronounced to be good. But Mr. Perkins, who had taken his seat among the humbler individuals, and in the very middle of the table, observed that all these persons, after drinking, made to each other very wry and ominous faces, and whispered much. He tasted his wine: it was a villanous compound of sugar, vitriol, soda-water, and green gooseberries. At this moment a great clatter of forks was made by the president's and vice-president's party. Silence for a toast—'twas silence all.

"Landlord," said Mr. Perkins, starting up (the rogue, where did his impudence come from?) "have you any champagne of YOUR OWN?"

"Silence! down!" roared the Tories, the ladies looking aghast. "Silence, sit down you!" shrieked the well-known voice of the General.

"I beg your pardon, General," said young John Perkins; "but where COULD you have bought this champagne? My worthy friend I know is going to propose the ladies; let us at any rate drink such a toast in good wine." ("Hear, hear!") "Drink her Ladyship's health in THIS stuff? I declare to goodness I would sooner drink it in beer!"

No pen can describe the uproar which arose: the anguish of the Gorgonites—the shrieks, jeers, cheers, ironic cries of "Swipes!" etc., which proceeded from the less genteel but more enthusiastic Scullyites.

"This vulgarity is too much," said Lady Gorgon, rising; and Mrs. Mayoress and the ladies of the party did so too.

The General, two squires, the clergyman, the Gorgon apothecary and attorney, with their respective ladies, followed her: they were plainly beaten from the field. Such of the Tories as dared remained, and in inglorious compromise shared the jovial Whig feast.

"Gentlemen and ladies," hiccupped Mr. Heeltap, "I'll give you a toast. 'Champagne to our real—hic—friends,' no, 'Real champagne to our friends,' and—hic—pooh! 'Champagne to our friends, and real pain to our enemies,'—huzzay!"

The Scully faction on this day bore the victory away, and if the polite reader has been shocked by certain vulgarities on the part of Mr. Scully and his friends, he must remember imprimis that Oldborough was an inconsiderable place—that the inhabitants thereof were chiefly tradespeople, not of refined habits—that Mr. Scully himself had only for three months mingled among the aristocracy—that his young friend Perkins was violently angry—and finally, and to conclude, that the proud vulgarity of the great Sir

George Gorgon and his family was infinitely more odious and contemptible than the mean vulgarity of the Scullyites and their leader.

Immediately after this event, Mr. Scully and his young friend Perkins returned to town; the latter to his garrets in Bedford Row—the former to his apartments on the first floor of the same house. He lived here to superintend his legal business: his London agents, Messrs. Higgs, Biggs, and Blatherwick, occupying the ground floor; the junior partner, Mr. Gustavus Blatherwick, the second flat of the house. Scully made no secret of his profession or residence: he was an attorney, and proud of it; he was the grandson of a labourer, and thanked God for it; he had made his fortune by his own honest labour, and why should he be ashamed of it?

And now, having explained at full length who the several heroes and heroines of this history were, and how they conducted themselves in the country, let us describe their behaviour in London, and the great events which occurred there.

You must know that Mr. Perkins bore away the tenderest recollections of the young lady with whom he had danced at the Oldborough ball, and, having taken particular care to find out where she dwelt when in the metropolis, managed soon to become acquainted with Aunt Biggs, and made himself so amiable to that lady, that she begged he would pass all his disengaged evenings at her lodgings in Caroline Place. Mrs. Biggs was perfectly aware that the young gentleman did not come for her bohea and muffins, so much as for the sweeter conversation of her niece, Miss Gorgon; but seeing that these two young people were of an age when ideas of love and marriage will spring up, do what you will; seeing that her niece had a fortune, and Mr. Perkins had the prospect of a place, and was moreover a very amiable and well-disposed young fellow, she thought her niece could not do better than marry him; and Miss Gorgon thought so too. Now the public will be able to understand the meaning of that important conversation which is recorded at the very commencement of this history.

Lady Gorgon and her family were likewise in town; but, when in the metropolis, they never took notice of their relative, Miss Lucy: the idea of acknowledging an ex-schoolmistress living in Mecklenburgh Square being much too preposterous for a person of my Lady Gorgon's breeding and fashion. She did not, therefore, know of the progress which sly Perkins was making all this while; for Lucy Gorgon did not think it was at all necessary to inform her Ladyship how deeply she was smitten by the wicked young gentleman who had made all the disturbance at the Oldborough ball.

The intimacy of these young persons had, in fact, become so close, that on a certain sunshiny Sunday in December, after having accompanied Aunt Biggs to church, they had pursued their walk as far as that rendezvous of lovers, the Regent's Park, and were talking of their coming marriage, with much confidential tenderness, before the bears in the Zoological Gardens.

Miss Lucy was ever and anon feeding those interesting animals with buns, to perform which act of charity she had clambered up on the parapet which surrounds their den. Mr. Perkins was below; and Miss Lucy, having distributed her buns, was on the point of following,—but whether from timidity, or whether from a desire to do young Perkins an essential service, I know not: however, she found herself quite unwilling to jump down unaided.

"My dearest John," said she, "I never can jump that."

Whereupon John stepped up, put one hand round Lucy's waist; and as one of hers gently fell upon his shoulder, Mr. Perkins took the other and said,—

"Now jump."

Hoop! jump she did, and so excessively active and clever was Mr. John Perkins, that he jumped Miss Lucy plump into the middle of a group formed of—

Lady Gorgon;

The Misses Gorgon;

Master George Augustus Frederick Grimsby Gorgon;

And a footman, poodle, and French governess: who had all been for two or three minutes listening to the billings and cooings of these imprudent young lovers.

CHAPTER II

SHOWS HOW THE PLOT BEGAN TO THICKEN IN OR ABOUT BEDFORD ROW

"Miss Lucy!"

"Upon my word!"

"I'm hanged if it aren't Lucy! How do, Lucy?" uttered Lady, the Misses, and Master Gorgon in a breath.

Lucy came forward, bending down her ambrosial curls, and blushing, as a modest young woman should: for, in truth, the scrape was very awkward. And as for John Perkins, he made a start, and then a step forwards, and then two backwards, and then began laying hands upon his black satin stock—in short, the sun did not shine at that moment upon a man who looked so exquisitely foolish.

"Miss Lucy Gorgon, is your aunt—is Mrs. Briggs here?" said Lady Gorgon, drawing herself up with much state.

"Mrs. Biggs, Aunt?" said Lucy demurely.

"Biggs or Briggs, madam, it is not of the slightest consequence. I presume that persons in my rank of life are not expected to know everybody's name in Magdeburg Square?" (Lady Gorgon had a house in Baker Street, and a dismal house it was.) "NOT here," continued she, rightly interpreting Lucy's silence, "NOT here?—and may I ask how long is it that young ladies have been allowed to walk abroad without chaperons, and to—to take a part in such scenes as that which we have just seen acted?"

To this question—and indeed it was rather difficult to answer—Miss Gorgon had no reply. There were the six grey eyes of her cousins glowering at her; there was George Augustus Frederick examining her with an air of extreme wonder, Mademoiselle the governess turning her looks demurely away, and awful Lady Gorgon glancing fiercely at her in front. Not mentioning the footman and poodle, what could a poor modest timid girl plead before such an inquisition, especially when she was clearly guilty? Add to this, that as Lady Gorgon, that majestic woman, always remarkable for her size and insolence of demeanour, had planted herself in the middle of the path, and spoke at the extreme pitch of her voice, many persons walking in the neighbourhood had heard her Ladyship's speech and stopped, and seemed disposed to await the rejoinder.

"For Heaven's sake, Aunt, don't draw a crowd around us," said Lucy, who, indeed, was glad of the only escape that lay in her power. "I will tell you of the—of the circumstances of—of my engagement with this gentleman—with Mr. Perkins," added she, in a softer tone—so soft that the 'ERKINS was quite inaudible.

"A Mr. What? An engagement without consulting your guardians!" screamed her Ladyship. "This must be looked to! Jerningham, call round my carriage. Mademoiselle, you will have the goodness to walk home with Master Gorgon, and carry him, if you please, where there is wet; and, girls, as the day is fine, you will do likewise. Jerningham, you will attend the young ladies. Miss Gorgon, I will thank you to follow me immediately." And so saying, and looking at the crowd with ineffable scorn, and at Mr. Perkins not at all, the lady bustled away forwards, the files of Gorgon daughters and governess closing round and enveloping poor Lucy, who found herself carried forward against her will, and in a minute seated in her aunt's coach, along with that tremendous person.

Her case was bad enough, but what was it to Perkins's? Fancy his blank surprise and rage at having his love thus suddenly ravished from him, and his delicious tete-a-tete interrupted. He managed, in an inconceivably short space of time, to conjure up half-a-million obstacles to his union. What should he do? he would rush on to Baker Street, and wait there until his Lucy left Lady Gorgon's house.

He could find no vehicle in the Regent's Park, and was in consequence obliged to make his journey on foot. Of course, he nearly killed himself with running, and ran so quick, that he was just in time to see the two ladies step out of Lady Gorgon's carriage at her own house, and to hear Jerningham's fellow-footman roar to the Gorgonian coachman, "Half-past seven!" at which hour we are, to this day, convinced that Lady Gorgon was going out to dine. Mr. Jerningham's associate having banged to the door, with an insolent look towards Perkins, who was prying in with the most suspicious and indecent curiosity, retired, exclaiming, "That chap has a hi to our great-coats, I reckon!" and left John Perkins to pace the street and be miserable.

John Perkins then walked resolutely up and down dismal Baker Street, determined on an eclaircissement. He was for some time occupied in thinking how it was that the Gorgons were not at church, they who made such a parade of piety; and John Perkins smiled as he passed the chapel, and saw that two CHARITY SERMONS were to be preached that day—and therefore it was that General Gorgon read prayers to his family at home in the morning.

Perkins, at last, saw that little General, in blue frock-coat and spotless buff gloves, saunter scowling home; and half an hour before his arrival had witnessed the entrance of Jerningham, and the three gaunt Miss Gorgons, poodle, son-and-heir, and French governess, protected by him, into Sir George's mansion.

"Can she be going to stay all night?" mused poor John, after being on the watch for three hours: when presently, to his inexpressible delight, he saw a very dirty hackney-coach clatter up to the Gorgon door, out of which first issued the ruby plush breeches and stalwart calves of Mr. Jerningham; these were followed by his body, and then the gentleman, ringing modestly, was admitted.

Again the door opened: a lady came out, nor was she followed by the footman, who crossed his legs at the door-post and allowed her to mount the jingling vehicle as best she might. Mr. Jerningham had witnessed the scene in the Park Gardens, had listened to the altercation through the library keyhole, and had been mighty sulky at being ordered to call a coach for this young woman. He did not therefore deign to assist her to mount.

But there was ONE who did! Perkins was by the side of his Lucy: he had seen her start back and cry, "La, John!"—had felt her squeeze his arm—had mounted with her into the coach, and then shouted with a voice of thunder to the coachman, "Caroline Place, Mecklenburgh Square."

But Mr. Jerningham would have been much more surprised and puzzled if he had waited one minute longer, and seen this Mr. Perkins, who had so gallantly escaladed the hackney-coach, step out of it with the most mortified, miserable, chap-fallen countenance possible.

The fact is, he had found poor Lucy sobbing fit to break her heart, and instead of consoling her, as he expected, he only seemed to irritate her further: for she said, "Mr. Perkins—I beg—I insist, that you leave the carriage." And when Perkins made some movement (which, not being in the vehicle at the time, we have never been able to comprehend), she suddenly sprang from the back-seat and began pulling at a large piece of cord which communicated with the wrist of the gentleman driving; and, screaming to him at the top of her voice, bade him immediately stop.

This Mr. Coachman did, with a curious, puzzled, grinning air.

Perkins descended, and on being asked, "Vere ham I to drive the young 'oman, sir?" I am sorry to say muttered something like an oath, and uttered the above-mentioned words, "Caroline Place, Mecklenburgh Square," in a tone which I should be inclined to describe as both dogged and sheepish— very different from that cheery voice which he had used when he first gave the order.

Poor Lucy, in the course of those fatal three hours which had passed while Mr. Perkins was pacing up and down Baker Street, had received a lecture which lasted exactly one hundred and eighty minutes— from her aunt first, then from her uncle, whom we have seen marching homewards, and often from both together.

Sir George Gorgon and his lady poured out such a flood of advice and abuse against the poor girl, that she came away from the interview quite timid and cowering; and when she saw John Perkins (the sly rogue! how well he thought he had managed the trick!) she shrank from him as if he had been a demon of wickedness, ordered him out of the carriage, and went home by herself, convinced that she had committed some tremendous sin.

While, then, her coach jingled away to Caroline Place, Perkins, once more alone, bent his steps in the same direction. A desperate, heart-stricken man, he passed by the beloved's door, saw lights in the front drawing-room, felt probably that she was there; but he could not go in. Moodily he paced down Doughty Street, and turning abruptly into Bedford Row, rushed into his own chambers, where Mrs. Snooks, the laundress, had prepared his humble Sabbath meal.

A cheerful fire blazed in his garret, and Mrs. Snooks had prepared for him the favourite blade-bone he loved (blest four-days' dinner for a bachelor—roast, cold, hashed, grilled bladebone, the fourth being better than the first); but although he usually did rejoice in this meal—ordinarily, indeed, grumbling that there was not enough to satisfy him—he, on this occasion, after two mouthfuls, flung down his knife and fork, and buried his two claws in his hair.

"Snooks," said he at last, very moodily, "remove this d— mutton, give me my writing things, and some hot brandy-and-water."

This was done without much alarm: for you must know that Perkins used to dabble in poetry, and ordinarily prepare himself for composition by this kind of stimulus.

He wrote hastily a few lines.

"Snooks, put on your bonnet," said he, "and carry this—YOU KNOW WHERE!" he added, in a hollow, heart-breaking tone of voice, that affected poor Snooks almost to tears. She went, however, with the note, which was to this purpose:—

"Lucy! Lucy! my soul's love—what, what has happened? I am writing this"—(a gulp of brandy-and-water)—"in a state bordering on distraction—madness—insanity" (another). "Why did you send me out of the coach in that cruel cruel way? Write to me a word, a line—tell me, tell me, I may come to you—and leave me not in this agonising condition; your faithful" (glog—glog—glog—the whole glass)—"J.P."

He never signed John Perkins in full—he couldn't, it was so unromantic.

Well, this missive was despatched by Mrs. Snooks, and Perkins, in a fearful state of excitement, haggard, wild, and with more brandy-and-water, awaited the return of his messenger.

When at length, after about an absence of forty years, as it seemed to him, the old lady returned with a large packet, Perkins seized it with a trembling hand, and was yet more frightened to see the handwriting of Mrs. or Miss Biggs.

"MY DEAR MR. PERKINS," she began—"Although I am not your soul's adored, I performed her part for once, since I have read your letter, as I told her. You need not be very much alarmed, although Lucy is at this moment in bed and unwell: for the poor girl has had a sad scene at her grand uncle's house in Baker Street, and came home very much affected. Rest, however, will restore her, for she is not one of your nervous sort; and I hope when you come in the morning, you will see her as blooming as she was when you went out to-day on that unlucky walk.

"See what Sir George Gorgon says of us all! You won't challenge him, I know, as he is to be your uncle, and so I may show you his letter.

"Good-night, my dear John. Do not go QUITE distracted before morning; and believe me your loving aunt, "JEMIMA BIGGS."

"41 BAKER STREET: 11th December.

"MAJOR-GENERAL SIR GEORGE GORGON has heard with the utmost disgust and surprise of the engagement which Miss Lucy Gorgon has thought fit to form.

"The Major-General cannot conceal his indignation at the share which Miss Biggs has taken in this disgraceful transaction.

"Sir George Gorgon puts an absolute veto upon all further communication between his niece and the low-born adventurer who has been admitted into her society, and begs to say that Lieutenant Fitch, of the Lifeguards, is the gentleman who he intends shall marry Miss Gorgon.

"It is the Major-General's wish, that on the 28th Miss Gorgon should be ready to come to his house, in Baker Street, where she will be more safe from impertinent intrusions than she has been in Mucklebury Square.

"MRS. BIGGS, "Caroline Place, "Mecklenburgh Square."

When poor John Perkins read this epistle, blank rage and wonder filled his soul, at the audacity of the little General, who thus, without the smallest title in the world, pretended to dispose of the hand and fortune of his niece. The fact is, that Sir George had such a transcendent notion of his own dignity and station, that it never for a moment entered his head that his niece, or anybody else connected with him, should take a single step in life without previously receiving his orders; and Mr. Fitch, a baronet's son, having expressed an admiration of Lucy, Sir George had determined that his suit should be accepted, and really considered Lucy's preference of another as downright treason.

John Perkins determined on the death of Fitch as the very least reparation that should satisfy him; and vowed too that some of the General's blood should be shed for the words which he had dared to utter.

We have said that William Pitt Scully, Esquire, M.P., occupied the first floor of Mr. Perkins's house in Bedford Row: and the reader is further to be informed that an immense friendship had sprung up between these two gentlemen. The fact is, that poor John was very much flattered by Scully's notice, and began in a very short time to fancy himself a political personage; for he had made several of Scully's speeches, written more than one letter from him to his constituents, and, in a word, acted as his gratis clerk. At least a guinea a week did Mr. Perkins save to the pockets of Mr. Scully, and with hearty good will too, for he adored the great William Pitt, and believed every word that dropped from the pompous lips of that gentleman.

Well, after having discussed Sir George Gorgon's letter, poor Perkins, in the utmost fury of mind that his darling should be slandered so, feeling a desire for fresh air, determined to descend to the garden and smoke a cigar in that rural quiet spot. The night was very calm. The moonbeams slept softly upon the herbage of Gray's Inn gardens, and bathed with silver splendour Theobald's Row. A million of little frisky twinkling stars attended their queen, who looked with bland round face upon their gambols, as they peeped in and out from the azure heavens. Along Gray's Inn wall a lazy row of cabs stood listlessly, for who would call a cab on such a night? Meanwhile their drivers, at the alehouse near, smoked the short pipe or quaffed the foaming beer. Perhaps from Gray's Inn Lane some broken sounds of Irish revelry might rise. Issuing perhaps from Raymond Buildings gate, six lawyers' clerks might whoop a tipsy song— or the loud watchman yell the passing hour; but beyond this all was silence; and young Perkins, as he sat in the summerhouse at the bottom of the garden, and contemplated the peaceful heaven, felt some influences of it entering into his soul, and almost forgetting revenge, thought but of peace and love.

Presently, he was aware there was someone else pacing the garden. Who could it be?—Not Blatherwick, for he passed the Sabbath with his grandmamma at Clapham; not Scully surely, for he always went to Bethesda Chapel, and to a select prayer-meeting afterwards. Alas! it WAS Scully; for though that gentleman SAID that he went to chapel, we have it for a fact that he did not always keep his promise, and was at this moment employed in rehearsing an extempore speech, which he proposed to deliver at St. Stephen's.

"Had I, sir," spouted he, with folded arms, slowly pacing to and fro—"Had I, sir, entertained the smallest possible intention of addressing the House on the present occasion—hum, on the present occasion—I would have endeavoured to prepare myself in a way that should have at least shown my sense of the greatness of the subject before the House's consideration, and the nature of the distinguished audience I have the honour to address. I am, sir, a plain man—born of the people—myself one of the people, having won, thank Heaven, an honourable fortune and position by my own honest labour; and standing here as I do—"

Here Mr. Scully (it may be said that he never made a speech without bragging about himself: and an excellent plan it is, for people cannot help believing you at last)—here, I say, Mr. Scully, who had one arm raised, felt himself suddenly tipped on the shoulder, and heard a voice saying, "Your money or your life!"

The honourable gentleman twirled round as if he had been shot; the papers on which a great part of this impromptu was written dropped from his lifted hand, and some of them were actually borne on the air into neighbouring gardens. The man was, in fact, in the direst fright.

"It's only I," said Perkins, with rather a forced laugh, when he saw the effect that his wit had produced.

"Only you! And pray what the dev—what right have you to—to come upon a man of my rank in that way, and disturb me in the midst of very important meditations?" asked Mr. Scully, beginning to grow fierce.

"I want your advice," said Perkins, "on a matter of the very greatest importance to me. You know my idea of marrying?"

"Marry!" said Scully; "I thought you had given up that silly scheme. And how, pray, do you intend to live?"

"Why, my intended has a couple of hundreds a year, and my clerkship in the Tape and Sealing-Wax Office will be as much more."

"Clerkship—Tape and Sealing-Wax Office—Government sinecure!—Why, good heavens! John Perkins, you don't tell ME that you are going to accept any such thing?"

"It is a very small salary, certainly," said John, who had a decent notion of his own merits; "but consider, six months vacation, two hours in the day, and those spent over the newspapers. After all, it's—"

"After all it's a swindle," roared out Mr. Scully—"a swindle upon the country; an infamous tax upon the people, who starve that you may fatten in idleness. But take this clerkship in the Tape and Sealing-Wax

Office," continued the patriot, his bosom heaving with noble indignation, and his eye flashing the purest fire,—"TAKE this clerkship, John Perkins, and sanction tyranny, by becoming one of its agents; sanction dishonesty by sharing in its plunder—do this, BUT never more be friend of mine. Had I a child," said the patriot, clasping his hands and raising his eyes to heaven, "I would rather see him dead, sir—dead, dead at my feet, than the servant of a Government which all honest men despise." And here, giving a searching glance at Perkins, Mr. Scully began tramping up and down the garden in a perfect fury.

"Good heavens!" exclaimed the timid John Perkins—"don't say SO. My dear Mr. Scully, I'm not the dishonest character you suppose me to be—I never looked at the matter in this light. I'll—I'll consider of it. I'll tell Crampton that I will give up the place; but for Heaven's sake, don't let me forfeit YOUR friendship, which is dearer to me than any place in the world."

Mr. Scully pressed his hand, and said nothing; and though their interview lasted a full half-hour longer, during which they paced up and down the gravel walk, we shall not breathe a single syllable of their conversation, as it has nothing to do with our tale.

The next morning, after an interview with Miss Lucy, John Perkins, Esquire, was seen to issue from Mrs. Biggs's house, looking particularly pale, melancholy, and thoughtful; and he did not stop until he reached a certain door in Downing Street, where was the office of a certain great Minister, and the offices of the clerks in his Lordship's department.

The head of them was Mr. Josiah Crampton, who has now to be introduced to the public. He was a little old gentleman, some sixty years of age, maternal uncle to John Perkins; a bachelor, who had been about forty-two years employed in the department of which he was now the head.

After waiting four hours in an ante-room, where a number of Irishmen, some newspaper editors, many pompous-looking political personages asking for the "first lord," a few sauntering clerks, and numbers of swift active messengers passed to and fro;—after waiting for four hours, making drawings on the blotting-book, and reading the Morning Post for that day week, Mr. Perkins was informed that he might go into his uncle's room, and did so accordingly.

He found a little hard old gentleman seated at a table covered with every variety of sealing-wax, blotting-paper, envelopes, despatch-boxes, green tapers, etc. etc. An immense fire was blazing in the grate, an immense sheet-almanack hung over that, a screen, three or four chairs, and a faded Turkey carpet, formed the rest of the furniture of this remarkable room—which I have described thus particularly, because in the course of a long official life, I have remarked that such is the invariable decoration of political rooms.

"Well, John," said the little hard old gentleman, pointing to an arm-chair, "I'm told you've been here since eleven. Why the deuce do you come so early?"

"I had important business," answered Mr. Perkins, stoutly; and as his uncle looked up with a comical expression of wonder, John began in a solemn tone to deliver a little speech which he had composed, and which proved him to be a very worthy, easy, silly fellow.

"Sir," said Mr. Perkins, "you have known for some time past the nature of my political opinions, and the intimacy which I have had the honour to form with one—with some of the leading members of the Liberal party." (A grin from Mr. Crampton.) "When first, by your kindness, I was promised the clerkship in the Tape and Sealing-Wax Office, my opinions were not formed as they are now; and having taken the advice of the gentlemen with whom I act,"—(an enormous grin)—"the advice, I say, of the gentlemen with whom I act, and the counsel likewise of my own conscience, I am compelled, with the deepest grief, to say, my dear uncle, that I—I—"

"That you—what, sir?" exclaimed little Mr. Crampton, bouncing off his chair. "You don't mean to say that you are such a fool as to decline the place?"

"I do decline the place," said Perkins, whose blood rose at the word "fool." "As a man of honour, I cannot take it."

"Not take it! and how are you to live? On the rent of that house of yours? For, by gad, sir, if you give up the clerkship, I never will give you a shilling."

"It cannot be helped," said Mr. Perkins, looking as much like a martyr as he possibly could, and thinking himself a very fine fellow. "I have talents, sir, which I hope to cultivate; and am member of a profession by which a man may hope to rise to the very highest offices of the State."

"Profession, talents, offices of the State! Are you mad, John Perkins, that you come to me with such insufferable twaddle as this? Why, do you think if you HAD been capable of rising at the bar, I would have taken so much trouble about getting you a place? No, sir; you are too fond of pleasure, and bed, and tea-parties, and small-talk, and reading novels, and playing the flute, and writing sonnets. You would no more rise at the bar than my messenger, sir. It was because I knew your disposition—that hopeless, careless, irresolute good-humour of yours—that I had determined to keep you out of danger, by placing you in a snug shelter, where the storms of the world would not come near you. You must have principles forsooth! and you must marry Miss Gorgon, of course: and by the time you have gone ten circuits, and had six children, you will have eaten up every shilling of your wife's fortune, and be as briefless as you are now. Who the deuce has put all this nonsense into your head? I think I know."

Mr. Perkins's ears tingled as these hard words saluted them; and he scarcely knew whether he ought to knock his uncle down, or fall at his feet and say, "Uncle, I have been a fool, and I know it." The fact is, that in his interview with Miss Gorgon and her aunt in the morning, when he came to tell them of the resolution he had formed to give up the place, both the ladies and John himself had agreed, with a thousand rapturous tears and exclamations, that he was one of the noblest young men that ever lived, had acted as became himself, and might with perfect propriety give up the place, his talents being so prodigious that no power on earth could hinder him from being Lord Chancellor. Indeed, John and Lucy had always thought the clerkship quite beneath him, and were not a little glad, perhaps, at finding a pretext for decently refusing it. But as Perkins was a young gentleman whose candour was such that he was always swayed by the opinions of the last speaker, he did begin to feel now the truth of his uncle's statements, however disagreeable they might be.

Mr. Crampton continued:—

"I think I know the cause of your patriotism. Has not William Pitt Scully, Esquire, had something to do with it?"

Mr. Perkins COULD not turn any redder than he was, but confessed with deep humiliation that "he HAD consulted Mr. Scully among other friends."

Mr. Crampton smiled—drew a letter from a heap before him, and tearing off the signature, handed over the document to his nephew. It contained the following paragraphs:—

"Hawksby has sounded Scully: we can have him any day we want him. He talks very big at present, and says he would not take anything under a... This is absurd. He has a Yorkshire nephew coming up to town, and wants a place for him. There is one vacant in the Tape Office, he says: have you not a promise of it?"

"I can't—I can't believe it," said John; "this, sir, is some weak invention of the enemy. Scully is the most honourable man breathing."

"Mr. Scully is a gentleman in a very fair way to make a fortune," answered Mr. Crampton. "Look you, John—it is just as well for your sake that I should give you the news a few weeks before the papers, for I don't want you to be ruined, if I can help it, as I don't wish to have you on my hands. We know all the particulars of Scully's history. He was a Tory attorney at Oldborough; he was jilted by the present Lady Gorgon, turned Radical, and fought Sir George in his own borough. Sir George would have had the peerage he is dying for, had he not lost that second seat (by-the-by, my Lady will be here in five minutes), and Scully is now quite firm there. Well, my dear lad, we have bought your incorruptible Scully. Look here,"—and Mr. Crampton produced three Morning Posts.

"'THE HONOURABLE HENRY HAWKSBY'S DINNER-PARTY.—Lord So-and-So—Duke of So-and-So—W. Pitt Scully, Esq. M.P.'

"Hawksby is our neutral, our dinner-giver.

"'LADY DIANA DOLDRUM'S ROUT.—W. Pitt Scully, Esq,' again.

"'THE EARL OF MANTRAP'S GRAND DINNER.'—A Duke—four Lords—'Mr. Scully, and Sir George Gorgon.'"

"Well, but I don't see how you have bought him; look at his votes."

"My dear John," said Mr. Crampton, jingling his watch-seals very complacently, "I am letting you into fearful secrets. The great common end of party is to buy your opponents—the great statesman buys them for nothing."

Here the attendant genius of Mr. Crampton made his appearance, and whispered something, to which the little gentleman said, "Show her Ladyship in,"—when the attendant disappeared.

"John," said Mr. Crampton, with a very queer smile, "you can't stay in this room while Lady Gorgon is with me; but there is a little clerk's room behind the screen there, where you can wait until I call you."

John retired, and as he closed the door of communication, strange to say, little Mr. Crampton sprang up and said, "Confound the young ninny, he has shut the door!"

Mr. Crampton then, remembering that he wanted a map in the next room, sprang into it, left the door half open in coming out, and was in time to receive Her Ladyship with smiling face as she, ushered by Mr. Strongitharm, majestically sailed in.

CHAPTER III

BEHIND THE SCENES

In issuing from and leaving open the door of the inner room, Mr. Crampton had bestowed upon Mr. Perkins a look so peculiarly arch, that even he, simple as he was, began to imagine that some mystery was about to be cleared up, or some mighty matter to be discussed. Presently he heard the well-known voice of Lady Gorgon in conversation with his uncle. What could their talk be about? Mr. Perkins was dying to know, and—shall we say it?—advanced to the door on tiptoe and listened with all his might.

Her Ladyship, that Juno of a woman, if she had not borrowed Venus's girdle to render herself irresistible, at least had adopted a tender, coaxing, wheedling, frisky tone, quite different from her ordinary dignified style of conversation. She called Mr. Crampton a naughty man, for neglecting his old friends, vowed that Sir George was quite hurt at his not coming to dine—nor fixing a day when he would come—and added, with a most engaging ogle, that she had three fine girls at home, who would perhaps make an evening pass pleasantly, even to such a gay bachelor as Mr. Crampton.

"Madam," said he, with much gravity, "the daughters of such a mother must be charming; but I, who have seen your Ladyship, am, alas! proof against even them."

Both parties here heaved tremendous sighs and affected to be wonderfully unhappy about something.

"I wish," after a pause, said Lady Gorgon—"I wish, dear Mr. Crampton, you would not use that odious title 'my Ladyship:' you know it always makes me melancholy."

"Melancholy, my dear Lady Gorgon; and why?"

"Because it makes me think of another title that ought to have been mine—ours (I speak for dear Sir George's and my darling boy's sake, Heaven knows, not mine). What a sad disappointment it has been to my husband, that after all his services, all the promises he has had, they have never given him his peerage. As for me, you know—"

"For you, my dear madam, I know quite well that you care for no such bauble as a coronet, except in so far as it may confer honour upon those most dear to you—excellent wife and noble mother as you are. Heigho! what a happy man is Sir George!"

Here there was another pause, and if Mr. Perkins could have seen what was taking place behind the screen, he would have beheld little Mr. Crampton looking into Lady Gorgon's face, with as love-sick a Romeo-gaze as he could possibly counterfeit; while her Ladyship, blushing somewhat and turning her own grey gogglers up to heaven, received all his words for gospel, and sat fancying herself to be the best, most meritorious, and most beautiful creature in the three kingdoms.

"You men are terrible flatterers," continued she; "but you say right: for myself I value not these empty distinctions. I am growing old, Mr. Crampton,—yes, indeed, I am, although you smile so incredulously,—and let me add, that MY thoughts are fixed upon HIGHER things than earthly crowns. But tell me, you who are all in all with Lord Bagwig, are we never to have our peerage? His Majesty, I know, is not averse; the services of dear Sir George to a member of His Majesty's august family, I know, have been appreciated in the highest quarter. Ever since the peace we have had a promise. Four hundred pounds has Sir George spent at the Heralds' Office (I myself am of one of the most ancient families in the kingdom, Mr. Crampton), and the poor dear man's health is really ruined by the anxious sickening feeling of hope so long delayed."

Mr. Crampton now assumed an air of much solemnity.

"My dear Lady Gorgon," said he, "will you let me be frank with you, and will you promise solemnly that what I am going to tell you shall never be repeated to a single soul?"

Lady Gorgon promised.

"Well, then, since the truth you must know, you yourselves have been in part the cause of the delay of which you complain. You gave us two votes five years ago; you now only give us one. If Sir George were to go up to the Peers, we should lose even that one vote; and would it be common sense in us to incur such a loss? Mr. Scully, the Liberal, would return another Member of his own way of thinking; and as for the Lords, we have, you know, a majority there."

"Oh, that horrid man!" said Lady Gorgon, cursing Mr. Scully in her heart, and beginning to play a rapid tattoo with her feet, "that miscreant, that traitor, that—that attorney has been our ruin."

"Horrid man, if you please, but give me leave to tell you that the horrid man is not the sole cause of your ruin—if ruin you will call it. I am sorry to say that I do candidly think Ministers believe that Sir George Gorgon has lost his influence in Oldborough as much through his own fault as through Mr. Scully's cleverness."

"Our own fault! Good heavens! Have we not done everything—everything that persons of our station in the county could do, to keep those misguided men? Have we not remonstrated, threatened, taken away our custom from the Mayor, established a Conservative apothecary—in fact, done all that gentlemen could do? But these are such times, Mr. Crampton: the spirit of revolution is abroad, and the great families of England are menaced by democratic insolence."

This was Sir George Gorgon's speech always after dinner, and was delivered by his lady with a great deal of stateliness. Somewhat, perhaps, to her annoyance, Mr. Crampton only smiled, shook his head, and said—

"Nonsense, my dear Lady Gorgon—pardon the phrase, but I am a plain old man, and call things by their names. Now, will you let me whisper in your ear one word of truth? You have tried all sorts of remonstrances, and exerted yourself to maintain your influence in every way, except the right one, and that is—"

"What, in Heaven's name?"

"Conciliation. We know your situation in the borough. Mr. Scully's whole history, and, pardon me for saying so (but we men in office know everything), yours—"

Lady Gorgon's ears and cheeks now assumed the hottest hue of crimson. She thought of her former passages with Scully, and of the days when—but never mind when: for she suffered her veil to fall, and buried her head in the folds of her handkerchief. Vain folds! The wily little Mr. Crampton could see all that passed behind the cambric, and continued—

"Yes, madam, we know the absurd hopes that were formed by a certain attorney twenty years since. We know how, up to this moment, he boasts of certain walks—"

"With the governess—we were always with the governess!" shrieked out Lady Gorgon, clasping her hands. "She was not the wisest of women."

"With the governess, of course," said Mr. Crampton, firmly. "Do you suppose that any man dare breathe a syllable against your spotless reputation? Never, my dear madam; but what I would urge is this—you have treated your disappointed admirer too cruelly."

"What! the traitor who has robbed us of our rights?"

"He never would have robbed you of your rights if you had been more kind to him. You should be gentle, madam; you should forgive him—you should be friends with him."

"With a traitor, never!"

"Think what made him a traitor, Lady Gorgon; look in your glass, and say if there be not some excuse for him? Think of the feelings of the man who saw beauty such as yours—I am a plain man and must speak—virtue such as yours, in the possession of a rival. By heavens, madam, I think he was RIGHT to hate Sir George Gorgon! Would you have him allow such a prize to be ravished from him without a pang on his part?"

"He was, I believe, very much attached to me," said Lady Gorgon, quite delighted; "but you must be aware that a young man of his station in life could not look up to a person of my rank."

"Surely not: it was monstrous pride and arrogance in Mr. Scully. But que voulez-vous? Such is the world's way. Scully could not help loving you—who that knows you can? I am a plain man, and say what I think. He loves you still. Why make an enemy of him, who would at a word be at your feet? Dearest Lady Gorgon, listen to me. Sir George Gorgon and Mr. Scully have already met—their meeting was our contrivance. It is for our interest, for yours, that they should be friends. If there were two Ministerial Members for Oldborough, do you think your husband's peerage would be less secure? I am not at liberty to tell you all I know on this subject; but do, I entreat you, be reconciled to him."

And after a little more conversation, which was carried on by Mr. Crampton in the same tender way, this important interview closed, and Lady Gorgon, folding her shawl round her, threaded certain mysterious passages and found her way to her carriage in Whitehall.

"I hope you have not been listening, you rogue?" said Mr. Crampton to his nephew, who blushed most absurdly by way of answer. "You would have heard great State secrets, if you had dared to do so. That woman is perpetually here, and if peerages are to be had for the asking, she ought to have been a duchess by this time. I would not have admitted her but for a reason that I have. Go you now and ponder upon what you have heard and seen. Be on good terms with Scully, and, above all, speak not a word concerning our interview—no, not a word even to your mistress. By the way, I presume, sir, you will recall your resignation?"

The bewildered Perkins was about to stammer out a speech, when his uncle, cutting it short, pushed him gently out of the door.

At the period when the important events occurred which have been recorded here, parties ran very high, and a mighty struggle for the vacant Speakership was about to come on. The Right Honourable Robert Pincher was the Ministerial candidate, and Sir Charles Macabaw was patronised by the Opposition. The two Members for Oldborough of course took different sides, the baronet being of the Pincher faction, while Mr. William Pitt Scully strongly supported the Macabaw party.

It was Mr. Scully's intention to deliver an impromptu speech upon the occasion of the election, and he and his faithful Perkins prepared it between them: for the latter gentleman had wisely kept his uncle's counsel and his own and Mr. Scully was quite ignorant of the conspiracy that was brooding. Indeed, so artfully had that young Machiavel of a Perkins conducted himself, that when asked by his patron whether he had given up his place in the Tape and Sealing Wax Office, he replied that "he HAD tendered his resignation," but did not say one word about having recalled it.

"You were right, my boy, quite right," said Mr. Scully. "A man of uncompromising principles should make no compromise." And herewith he sat down and wrote off a couple of letters, one to Mr. Hawksby, telling him that the place in the Sealing-Wax Office was, as he had reason to know, vacant; and the other to his nephew, stating that it was to be his. "Under the rose, my dear Bob," added Mr. Scully, "it will cost you five hundred pounds; but you cannot invest your money better."

It is needless to state that the affair was to be conducted "with the strictest secrecy and honour," and that the money was to pass through Mr. Scully's hands.

While, however, the great Pincher and Macabaw question was yet undecided, an event occurred to Mr. Scully, which had a great influence upon his after-life. A second grand banquet was given at the Earl of Mantrap's: Lady Mantrap requested him to conduct Lady Gorgon to dinner; and the latter, with a charming timidity, and a gracious melancholy look into his face (after which her veined eyelids veiled her azure eyes), put her hand into the trembling one of Mr. Scully and said as much as looks could say, "Forgive and forget."

Down went Scully to dinner. There were dukes on his right hand and earls on his left; there were but two persons without title in the midst of that glittering assemblage; the very servants looked like noblemen. The cook had done wonders; the wines were cool and rich, and Lady Gorgon was splendid! What attention did everybody pay to her and to him! Why WOULD she go on gazing into his face with that tender imploring look? In other words, Scully, after partaking of soup and fish (he, during their discussion, had been thinking over all the former love-and-hate passages between himself and Lady Gorgon), turned very red, and began talking to her.

"Were you not at the opera on Tuesday?" began he, assuming at once the airs of a man of fashion. "I thought I caught a glimpse of you in the Duchess of Diddlebury's box."

"Opera, Mr. Scully?" (pronouncing the word "Scully" with the utmost softness). "Ah, no! we seldom go, and yet too often. For serious persons the enchantments of that place are too dangerous. I am so nervous—so delicate; the smallest trifle so agitates, depresses, or irritates me, that I dare not yield myself up to the excitement of music. I am too passionately attached to it; and, shall I tell you? it has such a strange influence upon me, that the smallest false note almost drives me to distraction, and for that very reason I hardly ever go to a concert or a ball."

"Egad," thought Scully, "I recollect when she would dance down a matter of five-and-forty couple, and jingle away at the 'Battle of Prague' all day."

She continued: "Don't you recollect, I do, with—oh, what regret!—that day at Oldborough race-ball, when I behaved with such sad rudeness to you? You will scarcely believe me, and yet I assure you 'tis the fact, the music had made me almost mad. Do let me ask your pardon for my conduct. I was not myself. Oh, Mr. Scully! I am no worldly woman; I know my duties, and I feel my wrongs. Nights and days have I lain awake weeping and thinking of that unhappy day—that I should ever speak so to an old friend; for we WERE old friends, were we not?"

Scully did not speak; but his eyes were bursting out of his head, and his face was the exact colour of a deputy-lieutenant's uniform.

"That I should ever forget myself and you so! How I have been longing for this opportunity to ask you to forgive me! I asked Lady Mantrap, when I heard you were to be here, to invite me to her party. Come, I know you will forgive me—your eyes say you will. You used to look so in old days, and forgive me my caprices THEN. Do give me a little wine—we will drink to the memory of old days."

Her eyes filled with tears; and poor Scully's hand caused such a rattling and trembling of the glass and the decanter that the Duke of Doldrum—who had been, during the course of this whispered sentimentality, describing a famous run with the Queen's hounds at the top of his voice—stopped at the jingling of the glass, and his tale was lost for ever. Scully hastily drank his wine, and Lady Gorgon turned round to her next neighbour, a little gentleman in black, between whom and herself certain conscious looks passed.

"I am glad poor Sir George is not here," said he, smiling.

Lady Gorgon said, "Pooh, for shame!" The little gentleman was no other than Josiah Crampton, Esquire, that eminent financier, and he was now going through the curious calculation before mentioned, by which you BUY A MAN FOR NOTHING. He intended to pay the very same price for Sir George Gorgon, too; but there was no need to tell the baronet so; only of this the reader must be made aware.

While Mr. Crampton was conducting this intrigue, which was to bring a new recruit to the Ministerial ranks, his mighty spirit condescended to ponder upon subjects of infinitely less importance, and to arrange plans for the welfare of his nephew and the young woman to whom he had made a present of his heart. These young persons, as we said before, had arranged to live in Mr. Perkins's own house in Bedford Row. It was of a peculiar construction, and might more properly be called a house and a half: for a snug little tenement of four chambers protruded from the back of the house into the garden. These rooms communicated with the drawing-rooms occupied by Mr. Scully; and Perkins, who acted as his friend and secretary, used frequently to sit in the one nearest the Member's study, in order that he might be close at hand to confer with that great man. The rooms had a private entrance too, were newly decorated, and in them the young couple proposed to live; the kitchen and garrets being theirs likewise.

What more could they need? We are obliged to be particular in describing these apartments, for extraordinary events occurred therein.

To say the truth, until the present period Mr. Crampton had taken no great interest in his nephew's marriage, or, indeed, in the young man himself. The old gentleman was of a saturnine turn, and inclined to undervalue the qualities of Mr. Perkins, which were idleness, simplicity, enthusiasm, and easy good-nature.

"Such fellows never do anything in the world," he would say, and for such he had accordingly the most profound contempt. But when, after John Perkins's repeated entreaties, he had been induced to make the acquaintance of Miss Gorgon, he became instantly charmed with her, and warmly espoused her cause against her overbearing relations.

At his suggestion she wrote back to decline Sir George Gorgon's peremptory invitation, and hinted at the same time that she had attained an age and a position which enabled her to be the mistress of her own actions. To this letter there came an answer from Lady Gorgon which we shall not copy, but which simply stated that Miss Lucy Gorgon's conduct was unchristian, ungrateful, unladylike, and immodest; that the Gorgon family disowned her for the future, and left her at liberty to form whatever base connections she pleased.

"A pretty world this," said Mr. Crampton, in a great rage, when the letter was shown to him. "This same fellow, Scully, dissuades my nephew from taking a place, because Scully wants it for himself. This prude of a Lady Gorgon cries out shame, and disowns an innocent amiable girl: she a heartless jilt herself once, and a heartless flirt now. The Pharisees, the Pharisees! And to call mine a base family, too!"

Now, Lady Gorgon did not in the least know Mr. Crampton's connection with Mr. Perkins, or she would have been much more guarded in her language; but whether she knew it or not, the old gentleman felt a huge indignation, and determined to have his revenge.

"That's right, Uncle! SHALL I call Gorgon out?" said the impetuous young Perkins, who was all for blood.

"John, you are a fool," said his uncle. "You shall have a better revenge: you shall be married from Sir George Gorgon's house, and you shall see Mr. William Pitt Scully sold for nothing." This to the veteran diplomatist seemed to be the highest triumph which man could possibly enjoy.

It was very soon to take place: and, as has been the case ever since the world began, woman, lovely woman was to be the cause of Scully's fall. The tender scene at Lord Mantrap's was followed by many others equally sentimental. Sir George Gorgon called upon his colleague the very next day, and brought with him a card from Lady Gorgon inviting Mr. Scully to dinner. The attorney eagerly accepted the invitation, was received in Baker Street by the whole amiable family with much respectful cordiality, and was pressed to repeat his visits as country neighbours should. More than once did he call, and somehow always at the hour when Sir George was away at his club, or riding in the Park, or elsewhere engaged. Sir George Gorgon was very old, very feeble, very much shattered in constitution. Lady Gorgon used to impart her fears to Mr. Scully every time he called there, and the sympathising attorney used to console her as best he might. Sir George's country agent neglected the property—his lady consulted Mr. Scully concerning it. He knew to a fraction how large her jointure was; how she was to have Gorgon Castle for her life; and how, in the event of the young baronet's death (he, too, was a sickly poor boy), the chief part of the estates, bought by her money, would be at her absolute disposal.

"What a pity these odious politics prevent me from having you for our agent," would Lady Gorgon say; and indeed Scully thought it was a pity too. Ambitious Scully! what wild notions filled his brain. He used to take leave of Lady Gorgon and ruminate upon these things; and when he was gone, Sir George and her Ladyship used to laugh.

"If we can but commit him—if we can but make him vote for Pincher," said the General, "my peerage is secure. Hawksby and Crampton as good as told me so."

The point had been urged upon Mr. Scully repeatedly and adroitly. "Is not Pincher a more experienced man than Macabaw?" would Sir George say to his guest over their wine. Scully allowed it. "Can't you vote for him on personal grounds, and say so in the House?" Scully wished he could—how he wished he could! Every time the General coughed, Scully saw his friend's desperate situation more and more, and thought how pleasant it would be to be lord of Gorgon Castle. "Knowing my property," cried Sir George, "as you do, and with your talents and integrity, what a comfort it would be could I leave you as guardian to my boy! But these cursed politics prevent it, my dear fellow. Why WILL you be a Radical?" And Scully cursed politics too. "Hang the low-bred rogue," added Sir George, when William Pitt Scully left the house: "he will do everything but promise."

"My dear General," said Lady Gorgon, sidling up to him and patting him on his old yellow cheek—"My dear Georgy, tell me one thing,—are you jealous?"

"Jealous, my dear! and jealous of THAT fellow—pshaw!"

"Well, then, give me leave, and you shall have the promise to-morrow."
To-morrow arrived. It was a remarkably fine day, and in the forenoon Mr. Perkins gave his accustomed knock at Scully's study, which was only separated from his own sitting-room by a double door. John had wisely followed his uncle's advice, and was on the best terms with the honourable Member.

"Here are a few sentences," said he, "which I think may suit your purpose. Great public services— undeniable merit—years of integrity—cause of reform, and Macabaw for ever!" He put down the paper. It was, in fact, a speech in favour of Mr. Macabaw.

"Hush," said Scully, rather surlily; for he was thinking how disagreeable it was to support Macabaw; and besides, there were clerks in the room, whom the thoughtless Perkins had not at first perceived. As soon as that gentleman saw them, "You are busy, I see," continued he in a lower tone. "I came to say that I must be off duty to-day, for I am engaged to take a walk with some ladies of my acquaintance."

So saying, the light-hearted young man placed his hat unceremoniously on his head, and went off through his own door, humming a song. He was in such high spirits that he did not even think of closing the doors of communication, and Scully looked after him with a sneer.

"Ladies, forsooth," thought he; "I know who they are. This precious girl that he is fooling with, for one, I suppose." He was right: Perkins was off on the wings of love, to see Miss Lucy; and she and Aunt Biggs and Uncle Crampton had promised this very day to come and look at the apartments which Mrs. John Perkins was to occupy with her happy husband.

"Poor devil," so continued Mr. Scully's meditations, "it is almost too bad to do him out of his place; but my Bob wants it, and John's girl has, I hear, seven thousand pounds. His uncle will get him another place before all that money is spent." And herewith Mr. Scully began conning the speech which Perkins had made for him.

He had not read it more than six times,—in truth, he was getting it by heart,—when his head clerk came to him from the front room, bearing a card: a footman had brought it, who said his lady was waiting below. Lady Gorgon's name was on the card! To seize his hat and rush downstairs was, with Mr. Scully, the work of an infinitesimal portion of time.

It was indeed Lady Gorgon in her Gorgonian chariot.

"Mr. Scully," said she, popping her head out of window and smiling in a most engaging way, "I want to speak to you, on something very particular INDEED"—and she held him out her hand. Scully pressed it most tenderly: he hoped all heads in Bedford Row were at the windows to see him. "I can't ask you into the carriage, for you see the governess is with me, and I want to talk secrets to you."

"Shall I go and make a little promenade?" said mademoiselle, innocently. And her mistress hated her for that speech.

"No. Mr. Scully, I am sure, will let me come in for five minutes?"

Mr. Scully was only too happy. My Lady descended and walked upstairs, leaning on the happy solicitor's arm. But how should he manage? The front room was consecrated to clerks; there were clerks too, as ill-luck would have it, in his private room. "Perkins is out for the day," thought Scully; "I will take her into his room." And into Perkins's room he took her—ay, and he shut the double doors after him too, and trembled as he thought of his own happiness.

"What a charming little study," said Lady Gorgon, seating herself. And indeed it was very pretty: for Perkins had furnished it beautifully, and laid out a neat tray with cakes, a cold fowl, and sherry, to entertain his party withal. "And do you bachelors always live so well?" continued she, pointing to the little cold collation.

Mr. Scully looked rather blank when he saw it, and a dreadful suspicion crossed his soul; but there was no need to trouble Lady Gorgon with explanations: therefore, at once, and with much presence of mind, he asked her to partake of his bachelor's fare (she would refuse Mr. Scully nothing that day). A pretty sight would it have been for young Perkins to see strangers so unceremoniously devouring his feast. She drank—Mr. Scully drank—and so emboldened was he by the draught that he actually seated himself by the side of Lady Gorgon, on John Perkins's new sofa.

Her Ladyship had of course something to say to him. She was a pious woman, and had suddenly conceived a violent wish for building a chapel of ease at Oldborough, to which she entreated him to subscribe. She enlarged upon the benefits that the town would derive from it, spoke of Sunday-schools, sweet spiritual instruction, and the duty of all well-minded persons to give aid to the scheme.

"I will subscribe a hundred pounds," said Scully, at the end of her Ladyship's harangue: "would I not do anything for you?"

"Thank you, thank you, dear Mr. Scully," said the enthusiastic woman. (How the "dear" went burning through his soul!) "Ah!" added she, "if you WOULD but do anything for me—if you, who are so eminently, so truly distinguished, in a religious point of view, would but see the truth in politics too; and if I could see your name among those of the true patriot party in this empire, how blest—oh! how blest should I be! Poor Sir George often says he should go to his grave happy, could he but see you the guardian of his boy; and I, your old friend (for we WERE friends, William), how have I wept to think of you as one of those who are bringing our monarchy to ruin. Do, do promise me this too!" And she took his hand and pressed it between hers.

The heart of William Pitt Scully, during this speech, was thumping up and down with a frightful velocity and strength. His old love, the agency of the Gorgon property—the dear widow—five thousand a year clear—a thousand delicious hopes rushed madly through his brain, and almost took away his reason. And there she sat—she, the loved one, pressing his hand and looking softly into his eyes.

Down, down he plumped on his knees.

"Juliana!" shrieked he, "don't take away your hand! My love—my only love!—speak but those blessed words again! Call me William once more, and do with me what you will."

Juliana cast down her eyes and said, in the very smallest type, "William!"—when the door opened, and in walked Mr. Crampton, leading Mrs. Biggs, who could hardly contain herself for laughing, and Mr. John Perkins, who was squeezing the arm of Miss Lucy. They had heard every word of the two last speeches.

For at the very moment when Lady Gorgon had stopped at Mr. Scully's door, the four above-named individuals had issued from Great James Street into Bedford Row.

Lucy cried out that it was her aunt's carriage, and they all saw Mr. Scully come out, bare-headed, in the sunshine, and my Lady descend, and the pair go into the house. They meanwhile entered by Mr. Perkins's own private door, and had been occupied in examining the delightful rooms on the ground-floor, which were to be his dining-room and library—from which they ascended a stair to visit the other two rooms, which were to form Mrs. John Perkins's drawing-room and bedroom. Now whether it was that they trod softly, or that the stairs were covered with a grand new carpet and drugget, as was the case, or that the party within were too much occupied in themselves to heed any outward disturbances, I know not; but Lucy, who was advancing with John (he was saying something about one of the apartments, the rogue!)—Lucy started and whispered, "There is somebody in the rooms!" and at that instant began the speech already reported, "THANK YOU, THANK YOU, DEAR MR. SCULLY," etc. etc., which was delivered by Lady Gorgon in a full clear voice; for, to do her Ladyship justice, SHE had not one single grain of love for Mr. Scully, and during the delivery of her little oration, was as cool as the coolest cucumber.

Then began the impassioned rejoinder, to which the four listened on the landing-place; and then the little "William," as narrated above: at which juncture Mr. Crampton thought proper to rattle at the door, and, after a brief pause, to enter with his party.

"William" had had time to bounce off his knees, and was on a chair at the other end of the room.

"What, Lady Gorgon!" said Mr. Crampton, with excellent surprise, "how delighted I am to see you! Always, I see employed in works of charity" (the chapel-of-ease paper was on her knees), "and on such an occasion, too,—it is really the most wonderful coincidence! My dear madam, here is a silly fellow, a nephew of mine, who is going to marry a silly girl, a niece of your own."

"Sir, I—" began Lady Gorgon, rising.

"They heard every word," whispered Mr. Crampton eagerly. "Come forward, Mr. Perkins, and show yourself." Mr. Perkins made a genteel bow. "Miss Lucy, please to shake hands with your aunt; and this, my dear madam, is Mrs. Biggs, of Mecklenburgh Square, who, if she were not too old, might marry a gentleman in the Treasury, who is your very humble servant." And with this gallant speech, old Mr. Crampton began helping everybody to sherry and cake.

As for William Pitt Scully, he had disappeared, evaporated, in the most absurd sneaking way imaginable. Lady Gorgon made good her retreat presently, with much dignity, her countenance undismayed, and her face turned resolutely to the foe.

About five days afterwards, that memorable contest took place in the House of Commons, in which the partisans of Mr. Macabaw were so very nearly getting him the Speakership. On the day that the report of the debate appeared in the Times, there appeared also an announcement in the Gazette as follows:—

"The King has been pleased to appoint John Perkins, Esquire, to be Deputy-Subcomptroller of His Majesty's Tape Office and Custos of the Sealing-Wax Department."

Mr. Crampton showed this to his nephew with great glee, and was chuckling to think how Mr. William Pitt Scully would be annoyed, who had expected the place, when Perkins burst out laughing and said, "By heavens, here is my own speech! Scully has spoken every word of it; he has only put in Mr. Pincher's name in the place of Mr. Macabaw's."

"He is ours now," responded his uncle, "and I told you WE WOULD HAVE HIM FOR NOTHING. I told you, too, that you should be married from Sir George Gorgon's, and here is proof of it."

It was a letter from Lady Gorgon, in which she said that, "had she known Mr. Perkins to be a nephew of her friend Mr. Crampton, she never for a moment would have opposed his marriage with her niece, and she had written that morning to her dear Lucy, begging that the marriage breakfast should take place in Baker Street."

"It shall be in Mecklenburgh Square," said John Perkins stoutly; and in Mecklenburgh Square it was.

William Pitt Scully, Esquire, was, as Mr. Crampton said, hugely annoyed at the loss of the place for his nephew. He had still, however, his hopes to look forward to, but these were unluckily dashed by the coming in of the Whigs. As for Sir George Gorgon, when he came to ask about his peerage, Hawksby told him that they could not afford to lose him in the Commons, for a Liberal Member would infallibly fill his place.

And now that the Tories are out and the Whigs are in, strange to say a Liberal does fill his place. This Liberal is no other than Sir George Gorgon himself, who is still longing to be a lord, and his lady is still devout and intriguing. So that the Members for Oldborough have changed sides, and taunt each other with apostasy, and hate each other cordially. Mr. Crampton still chuckles over the manner in which he tricked them both, and talks of those five minutes during which he stood on the landing-place, and hatched and executed his "Bedford-Row Conspiracy."

William Makepeace Thackeray, was born on July 18th, 1811 in Calcutta, then British India, where his father, Richmond Thackeray was the secretary to the Board of Revenue in the British East India Company. His mother, Anne Becher also worked for the British East India Company.

His father died in 1815, and his mother sent Thackeray to England the following year while she remained in India and would, sometime later, marry her childhood sweetheart. En-route to England the ship stopped for provisions on St. Helena. The Imprisoned Napoleon was pointed out to him by a servant with the words that he "eats three sheep every day, and all the little children he can lay hands on!"

Finally, back in England the young Thackeray was sent to school, initially in Southampton and Chiswick, before being moved to Charterhouse School. Charterhouse and Thackeray did not take to each other but the time became a valuable source for his later work "Slaughterhouse". Despite his less than respectful recalling of his time with them Charterhouse placed a monument in the chapel after his death.

In his final year at Charterhouse a troubling illness delayed his departure to attend Cambridge University. Over the course of his life Thackeray would suffer from ill health, much of it brought about for his fondness for "gluttling and gorging". Excess was something he could enjoy and for a man who stood some 6' 3" it would appear to the eye that, initially at least, his large frame could absorb much of that excess.

However, Thackeray's lazy attitude to completely mastering anything he set his mind too, especially where ambition for academia was involved, meant he departed Cambridge little more than a year after joining. He had however published two short works in University periodicals. As an author, he would have quite some impact on English literature in the years to come, so it seems difficult to reconcile that he felt no urgency to pursue writing at that time.

He now spent some time travelling across Europe stopping at both Paris, to study art, and to winter in Weimar. Back in London a final attempt was made on a professional career. This time studying law at Middle Temple. It lasted no more than a few months.

Now, having reached 21, he received his father's inheritance. It was a very substantial estate of 17,000 pounds, an enormous sum of money at the time. However, although Thackeray had youth he lacked a little in energy and certainly much financial experience. He funded not one but two newspapers, and neither was to prove successful. Gambling seemed enjoyable and certainly he had money to lose, which he did on a regular basis. Further investments in two soon-to-fail Indian banks quickly ensured little of his good fortune remained.

He now had to consider taking up yet another profession. Thackeray turned to art hoping that his studies in Paris would prove of benefit. Unfortunately, they did not. His ambivalent attitude continued until on August 20th, 1836 he married the 20-year-old, Isabella Gethin Shawe. It seemed to prove a turning point in many ways.

The marriage would produce three daughters; Anne Isabella in 1837, Jane, in 1838, who tragically died in infancy and Harriet Marian in 1840.

Now, as a husband and father, Thackeray seemed at last to understand his responsibilities to nurture and provide.

His early efforts at "writing for his life" were to establish his career as a foremost author. His main employment was with Fraser's Magazine, a sharp-witted and sharp-tongued conservative publication for which he produced art criticism, short fictional sketches, and who would also serialise two of his novels. He also found time, between 1837 and 1840 to review books for The Times and to make regular contributions to The Morning Chronicle and The Foreign Quarterly Review.

In his earliest works, which he wrote under various pseudonyms including; Charles James Yellowplush, Michael Angelo Titmarsh and George Savage Fitz-Boodle, he tended towards savagery in his attacks on high society, military prowess, the institution of marriage and hypocrisy.

Between May 1839 and February 1840 Fraser's published Catherine. Originally intended as a satire of the Newgate school of crime fiction, it ended up being more of a picaresque tale. Thackeray also began work on what would eventually become A Shabby Genteel Story.

However, Thackeray, having successfully found a career that he cared about and had the talent for, found that his personal life was about to descend into chaos. After the birth of her third child in 1840, Isabella, sank into depression. At first Thackeray, didn't think too much of it. He needed to work to earn an income to support his family and finding that Isabella was distracting both herself and him he realised he could get no work done at home and so spent more and more time away until finally, in September 1840, it dawned upon him how serious his wife's condition had become. Struck by guilt, he set out with his wife to Ireland. During the boat crossing she threw herself into the sea, but was thankfully pulled from the waters. Her mother who had little understanding of her daughter's illness was of little help and perhaps a hinderance. After four-weeks they returned to England. From November 1840 to February 1842 Isabella was in and out of professional care, as her condition waxed and waned.

Isabella eventually deteriorated into a permanent state of detachment. Thackeray desperately sought cures for her, but nothing worked, and she ended up in two different asylums in or near Paris until 1845, after which Thackeray took her back to England, where he installed her with a Mrs Bakewell at Camberwell. Despite her condition Isabella would outlive her husband by 3 decades.

After his wife's illness Thackeray became a de facto widower, never able to establish another permanent relationship.

In 1843, through his connection to the illustrator John Leech, whom he had met at Charterhouse, he began writing for the newly created magazine Punch, in which he published The Snob Papers, later collected as The Book of Snobs. Thackeray was a regular contributor to Punch until 1854.

Thackeray had earlier received some success with two travel books, The Paris Sketch Book and The Irish Sketch Book, the latter marked by hostility to Irish Catholics. The book appealed to British prejudices, and on that basis Thackeray now became Punch's Irish expert, often under the pseudonym Hibernis

Hibernior. It was Thackeray's writings that were the basis for Punch's notoriously harsh, hostile and condescending depictions of the Irish during the devastating Irish Famine (1845–51).

As well as his regular columns and contributions Thackeray worked on his novels. In The Luck of Barry Lyndon, which was serialised in Fraser's in 1844, he explored the situation of an outsider trying to achieve status in high society, a theme he developed more successfully a few years later with Vanity Fair.

Thackeray achieved more recognition with his Snob Papers (serialised 1846/7, and published as a book in 1848), but the work that really established his fame was the novel Vanity Fair, which first appeared in serialised instalments beginning in January 1847.

Published as a book the novel had a slow start but eventually sales rose to 7,000 copies a month. Just as importantly, it was the book that everybody was talking about. Thackeray finally had a name that gained notice and was reviewed in journals such as the famed, and much sought after, Edinburgh Review.

The accolades and success also gave him a respite from writing everything in a manner that would help ensure income rather than literary respect. Even before Vanity Fair completed its serial run Thackeray had become a celebrity, sought after by the very lords and ladies whom he satirised. with the character of Becky Sharp, the artist's daughter who rises high by manipulating all around her.

Pendennis followed in 1849-50, but it was interrupted halfway through writing for 3 months by a severe illness. Some accounts say it was cholera. Pendennis is a semi-autobiographical bildungsroman that draws on, among other things, Thackeray's disappointments in college, his ambivalent relationship with his mother, and his insider's knowledge of the London publishing world.

This novel ran at the same time as Charles Dicken's David Copperfield, and their dual appearance brought about the first of many comparisons with Dickens. Thackeray, for his part, felt that he and Dickens were battling for supremacy, though he would never equal Dickens's popularity, except with the critics.

Interestingly the two were involved in a spat which became known as the "Garrick Club affair". Thackeray and Dickens had skirmished over the "Dignity of Literature" and had other slight disagreements but this literary quarrel caused a rift in their friendship that lasted almost until the end of Thackeray's life. The relationship was healed only in Thackeray's last months, through a surprise meeting and handshake on the steps of a London club. Thackeray had taken offense at some personal remarks in a column by Edmund Yates and demanded an apology, eventually taking the affair to the Garrick Club committee. Already upset with Thackeray for an indiscreet remark about his affair with Ellen Ternan, Dickens championed Yates, helping him to write letters both to Thackeray and, in his defense, to the club's committee. Despite the intervention of Dickens, Yates eventually lost the vote of the Club's members, but the quarrel was laid out for the public in journal articles and pamphlets. "What pains me most," Thackeray said at the time, "is that Dickens should have been his adviser, and next that I should have had to lay a heavy hand on a young man who, I take it, has been cruelly punished by the issue of the affair, and I believe is hardly aware of the nature of his own offence, and doesn't even now understand that a gentleman should resent the monstrous insult which he volunteered".

Aside from these quarrelsome, distracting literary disagreements and Isabella's on-going illness life was good for Thackeray. He was to remain as he put it "at the top of the tree," for the rest of his life. The works for which he is so well remembered; Vanity Fair and Barry Lyndon had established that but he continued to write and produce novels, stories, sketches and works profusely.

To remain at such a high level in both quality and quantity is somewhat surprising given the continuation and escalation of various illnesses which continued to haunt him.

With Isabella still unwell Thackeray did seek out other women, in particular Mrs Jane Brookfield. Despite his hopes, it always felt that he was pursuing her as she battled the problems of her own marriage and turned to Thackeray for comfort and support. A source for these relationships often came on the lecture tours of Great Britain and the United States which he now entertained. These tours gave the public a chance to see and hear their hero's and provided another valuable source of income for those invited to tour. Whilst in in New York he met the Baxter family. Sally, the eldest daughter, enchanted the novelist—as a number of vibrant, intelligent, beautiful young women had done before her—and she became the model for Ethel Newcome. He visited her on his second tour of the States when she was married to a South Carolina gentleman. His choosing of married women in the shape of both Jane and Sally was ill-advised and both relationships led nowhere but did take quite some time to disassemble and for reason to set in.

In 1852, The History of Henry Esmond was published as a 3-volume novel without first being serialised and in a special type meant to imitate the appearance of an eighteenth-century book. This was the most carefully planned of Thackeray's novels. The book was celebrated for its brilliance, and Thackeray recognized it as "the very best I can do". At the time, it caused a sensation thanks to its controversial ending, wherein the hero marries a woman who early in the novel seemed more like a "mother" to him.

The eighteenth-century held a great attraction for Thackeray and he had previously set both Barry Lyndon and Catherine there as well as the sequel to Esmond, The Virginians, which takes place in North America and includes George Washington as a character.

Thackeray had twice visited the United States on lecture tours during this period as well as given lectures in London on the English humorists of the eighteenth century, and on the first four Hanoverian monarchs. The latter were published in a book as The Four Georges.

Interestingly Thackeray also decided that Politics was something he could more than dabble in. In Oxford he stood as an independent for Parliament. He was narrowly beaten by Cardwell, a politician who was substituted for the man Thackeray thought he was going to run against, although Thackeray's advocacy of entertainment on the Sabbath would have done little to help his campaign. Even so the margin of his defeat was only 1,070 votes, to Thackeray's 1,005.

In 1860 Thackeray became editor of the newly established Cornhill Magazine, a role he never felt truly comfortable in, preferring to contribute as a columnist on the Roundabout Papers. However, the financial compensation was by all accounts quite extraordinary. The Cornhill began its history with a record circulation and a number of distinguished contributors swayed onboard by Thackeray's reputation. It was in the Cornhill that he serialised his last complete novel, The Adventures of Philip in 1861-62. (After his death, the incomplete Denis Duval would also appear there in 1864).

After two years as editor he stepped down, primarily to concentrate on writing novels again. A piece he wrote for the Cornhill at this time "Thorns in the Cushion," one of The Roundabout Papers, fondly assembles the pains he felt in rejecting manuscripts on the one hand and receiving criticism of the magazine on the other. It seemed a good time to move on.

Thackeray's health had worsened during the 1850s and he was plagued by a recurring stricture of the urethra that laid him up for days at a time. He also felt that he had lost much of his creative impetus. He worsened matters by excessively eating and drinking, and avoiding exercise, though he enjoyed horseback-riding. He has been described as "the greatest literary glutton who ever lived". Indeed, his main activity apart from writing was eating and drinking and many of his stories include elaborate scenes and themes on his fondness for them.

On December 23rd, 1863, William Makepeace Thackeray, after returning from dining out and before dressing for bed, suffered a massive stroke. He was found dead on his bed the following morning. He was only fifty-two.

His death was entirely unexpected, and shocked family, friends and indeed the entire Nation.

It is said that at his funeral service thousands of mourners turned out to witness his passing. He was buried on December 29th at Kensal Green Cemetery, London.

William Makepeace Thackeray – A Concise Bibliography

The Yellowplush Papers (1837)
Catherine (1839–40)
A Shabby Genteel Story (1840)
Second Funeral of Napoleon (1841)
The Irish Sketchbook (1843)
The Luck of Barry Lyndon (1844)
Notes of a Journey from Cornhill to Grand Cairo (1846)
Mrs. Perkins's Ball (1846), under the name M. A. Titmarsh
Stray Papers: Being Stories, Reviews, Verses, and Sketches (1821-1847)
The Book of Snobs (1848)
Vanity Fair (1848)
Pendennis (1848–1850)
Rebecca and Rowena (1850)
The Paris Sketchbook (1840)
Men's Wives (1852)
The History of Henry Esmond (1852)
The English Humorists of the Eighteenth Century (1853)
The Newcomes (1855)
The Rose and the Ring (1855)
The Virginians (1857–1859)
Lovel the Widower (1860)
Four Georges (1860-1861)
The Adventures of Philip (1862)

Roundabout Papers (1863)
Denis Duval (1864)
The English Humorists of the eighteenth century: A Series of Six Lectures (1867)
Ballads (1869)
Burlesques (1869)
The Orphan of Pimlico (1876)

Thackeray wrote a numerous number of articles for magazines and the like as well as contributing many picture sketches to articles and his own books. Many were then collected and published together. We have listed his major works only for this bibliography.

www.ingramcontent.com/pod-product-compliance
Lightning Source LLC
Chambersburg PA
CBHW061506170626
46811CB00004B/1621